Hares to my agent,
EVELYNE JOHNSON!
It's her fault I did something bunny...er...punny.

Once upon a time there were three hares that lived in a cozy hole in the woods. There was a great big papa hare, a medium-sized mama hare, and a teeny tiny baby hare.

They each had a bowl for their oatmeal. The papa hare had a great big bowl. The mama hare had a medium-sized bowl. And the baby hare had a teeny tiny bowl.

So the three hares decided to eat out for breakfast.

Off they sped in their van. Meanwhile, a little girl named Goldilocks came bouncing down the forest path.

She peered down the hole, but she couldn't see her ball.

In the kitchen of the three hares, Goldilocks found the three bowls—the great big bowl, the medium-sized bowl, and the teeny tiny bowl.

Finally Goldilocks tried the oatmeal in the teeny tiny bowl. It was just right, so she gobbled it all up.

Then Goldilocks wandered into the family room and saw three chairs—a great big chair, a medium-sized chair, and a teeny tiny chair. First she sat in the great big chair.

The great big chair
was too hard to figure out.

So Goldilocks hobbled to the medium-sized chair.

The medium-sized chair went too fast.

Finally Goldilocks sat down in the teeny tiny chair. It was just right.

Then Goldilocks decided to see what was upstairs.

Upstairs, Goldilocks found three beds—a great big bed, a medium-sized bed, and a teeny tiny bed.

First she tried the great big waterbed. It was too hard to keep her breakfast down.

Next Goldilocks tried the medium-sized bed. It was too soft.

Finally she tried the teeny tiny bed. It was just right.

As soon as the police arrived, they checked the kitchen.

Next they checked the family room.

Why is this page so white?

Well, I couldn't think of a background— so I drew a blank!

Well, look at that—there's the copyright information!

I thought they'd forgotten it!

It's long, but not forgotten!

Did they copy it right?

If they saved the jest for last, this must be THE END!

Not quite. Let's check out the back cover!

Checkers, anyone?

ISBN 0-439-07777-X

Copyright © 1995 by Heidi Petach. All rights reserved.
Published by Scholastic Inc., 555 Broadway, New York, NY 10012, by arrangement with G. P. Putnam's Sons, a division of The Putnam & Grosset Group. SCHOLASTIC and associated logos are trademarks and/or registered trademarks of Scholastic Inc.

12 11 10 9 8 7 6 5 4 3 2 1   8 9/9 0 1 2 3/0

Printed in the U.S.A.   08

First Scholastic printing, February 1998